GAMAGO thanks all of the wonderful
people at Chronicle Books for their
hard work to make this book happen.
Special thanks to our editor, Naomi.

For my son, Jack.

-Greg

Text © 2013 by Greg Long and Chris Edmundson. Illustrations © 2013 by Wednesday Kirwan. All rights reserved. No part of this
book may be reproduced in any form without written permission from the publisher. • Library of Congress Cataloging-in-Publication
Data available. ISBN 978-1-4521-1158-2 • Book design by Ryan Hayes. Typeset in Router. The illustrations in this book were rendered
digitally. • Manufactured in China. • 10 9 8 7 6 5 4 3 • Chronicle Books LLC, 680 Second Street, San Francisco, California 94107
Chronicle Books—we see things differently. Become part of our community at www.chroniclekids.com.

yeti, Turn Out the Light!

By **Greg Long** & **Chris Edmundson**
Illustrated by **Wednesday Kirwan**

chronicle books · san francisco

From deep in the forest,
there comes a loud yawn.
It's Yeti . . . he's sleepy,
for the day's nearly gone.

So Yeti heads home, eats his dinner, and flosses.

Then he snuggles into bed, but he turns and he tosses.

"Why?" you may ask.
Well I'll tell you, my dear.
Yeti sees shadows
dart frightfully near!

They dance up the wall,
and, my, are they scary!

Oh, what could they be?
Yeti is wary . . .

On the light goes,
and to Yeti's surprise,
he sees only bunnies,
and their big bunny eyes.

Back in bed
with the bunnies,
Yeti feels sleepy.

Then he sits up and shouts,
"What's that shadow?! It's creepy!"

On the light goes!
But there's nothing to fear.
It's just three little birds
on top of a deer.

Yeti is flustered.
He needs milk to calm down.

But when he reaches the kitchen,
he hears a strange sound!

On the light goes!
Oh, what could it be?

Why, it's just Bear and Owl,
and they're drinking some tea!

Yeti tries to sleep
(with bunnies, birds, deer, bear, and owl),

but he soon sees a shadow
so frightfully foul!

On the light goes!
All the animals scatter.

But Yeti just laughs,
for there is nothing
the matter.

"The shadow is just *us*," Yeti says with a sigh. "It's time to go home, friends. Sweet dreams and good-bye."

With a bed to himself,
and the dark all around,

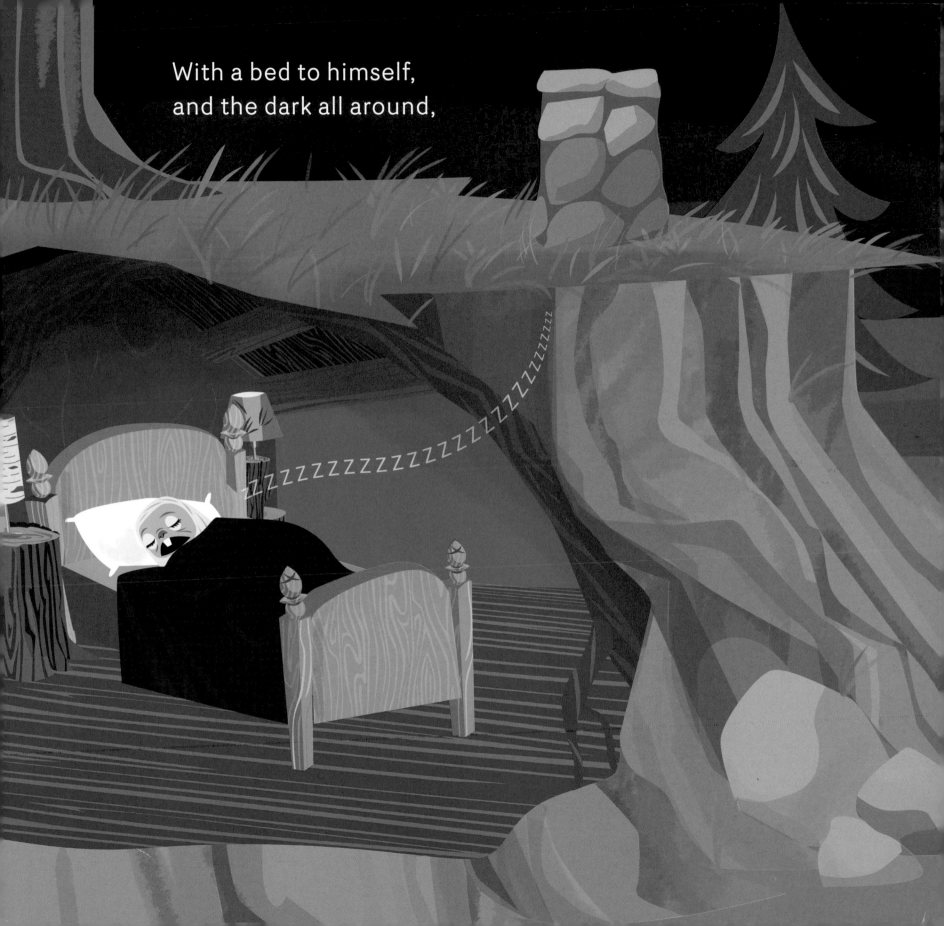

The zzzzz's Yeti yearned for are finally found.